DON'T FORGET THE BACON!

Pat Hutchins

Greenwillow Books
An Imprint of **HarperCollins***Publishers*

DON'T FORGET
THE BACON!

Don't Forget the Bacon!

For information address HarperCollins Children's Books, a division of HarperCollins Publishers, 10 East 53rd Street, New York, NY 10022.
www.harperchildrens.com

Library of Congress Cataloging-in-Publication Data
Hutchins, Pat
Don't forget the bacon! / by Pat Hutchins.
p. cm.
"Greenwillow Books."
Summary: A little boy goes grocery shopping for his mother and tries hard to remember her instructions.
ISBN 0-688-80019-X — ISBN 0-688-84019-1 (lib. bdg.)
ISBN 0-688-06787-5 (1987 Printing)
ISBN 0-688-06788-3 (lib bdg. 1987 Printing) — ISBN 0-688-08743-4 (pbk.)
[1. Stories in rhyme] I. Title.
PZ8.3.H965Do 75-17935
[E] CIP
AC

12 13 SCP 20 19 18 17

For Ben and Jeb Kidd

SIX FARM EGGS,
A CAKE FOR TEA,
A POUND OF PEARS,
AND DON'T FORGET
THE BACON.

six fat legs
a cake for tea
a pound of pears
and don't forget
the bacon

six fat legs
a cape for me
a pound of pears
and don't forget
the bacon

six fat legs
a cape for me
a flight of stairs
and don't forget
the bacon

six clothes pegs
a cape for me
a flight of stairs
and don't forget
the bacon

six clothes pegs
a rake for leaves
a flight of stairs
and don't forget
the bacon

Furniture
six clothes pegs
a rake for leaves
a pile of chairs
and don't forget
the bacon

Junk shop
Open
Letters

SIX CLOTHES PEGS,
A RAKE FOR LEAVES,
AND A PILE OF CHAIRS, PLEASE.
Sold
4·25
1·20

a pile of chairs?

a flight of stairs?

A POUND OF PEARS!

Homestead Farm Produce
Pears Apples Plums tel:
apples 15 lb.
Pears 20 lb
Plums 20 lb

a rake for leaves?

a cape for me?

A CAKE FOR TEA!

41 The Cake Shop 41
fresh cream cakes
41

six clothes pegs?

six fat legs?

SIX FARM EGGS!

laundry

six farm eggs,
a cake for tea,
and a pound of pears!

I FORGOT THE BACON!